# The Smelly P

John Cameron

GW00995253

A PICTURE CORGI

One morning Dan and his dog Napoleon were woken up early by the postman with a parcel. It was from his old friend Farmer Hendriks in Holland.

Inside was a note from Farmer Hendriks and a big bunch of bashed-up flowers.

THE WEIRDEST,
MOST WONDERFUL ZOO
IN THE WORLD

Menagerie Dan's Monster Zoo: The Smelly Pongeroos
A Picture Corgi 0 552 52400X

Designed and produced by
Genesis Productions Limited
30 Great Portland Street, London W1

First published in Great Britain 1986

Copyright © John Cameron 1986

Picture Corgi Books are published by
Transworld Publishers Limited
61–63 Uxbridge Road, Ealing, London W5 5SA

Printed and bound in Hong Kong by
Mandarin Offset Marketing (H.K.) Ltd.

Dan got dressed and began to put into his truck everything he might need to catch a Pongeroo. While he was packing he read hints from his big red monster-catching book.

It seems that Pongeroos are big and furry with a huge long nose and they love anything smelly.

Dan set sail for Holland that morning.

When Dan reached his friend's farm he realised why the bunch of flowers he had sent was all bashed-up.

There in the middle of Farmer Hendriks' flower field was a herd of Pongeroos tramping up and down on the flowers and sniffing the lovely scent with their huge pink hooters.

'I think I'll try my brand-new Pongeroo traps, Farmer Hendriks,' said Dan. 'They're made from specially adapted dustbins. What I'll do is bait them with some nice smelly cheese. When the Pongeroos come and shove their hooters in, I'll press this button here and the lids will shut tight and catch them.'

Carefully Dan pushed the traps in among the Pongeroos and hid himself.

The Pongeroos got a whiff of the stinky cheese and were just about to shove their noses in the traps when...

'A-tishoo!' Dan let out a sneeze.

The Pongeroos hopped off in fright and Dan pressed the button too late.

'Drat it!' said Dan. 'I think I'm getting hay fever with all these flowers!'

Dan packed everything into his truck and set off down the road after the Pongeroos.

He hadn't gone far when he met a terrified baker running the other way. 'Big furry monsters!' he shouted breathlessly. 'They're wrecking my bakery!'

Dan went with him to the bakery and found the Pongeroos stomping all over the newly-baked bread, breathing in the delicious smell.

'Aha!' said Dan. 'Now we've got them trapped.'

The baker stood guard while Dan got some equipment from his truck and built a big cage around the bakery door.

'What I'll do', explained Dan, 'is fix up this big vacuum cleaner to the back of the cage here and suck all the smells out of the bakery. The Pongeroos will follow the smells right into the cage. You slam the door when they're all in, and we'll have caught them.'

Everything was ready. The baker stood ready at the door, and Dan was just about to start the vacuum cleaner when...

'A-tishoo!' He sneezed and accidentally pushed the switch to blow instead of suck.

It blew so hard that it whooshed the Pongeroos right out of the back door of the bakery.

'Drat this hay fever!' said Dan. 'I'd better get after them.'

Dan couldn't believe his eyes when he saw where the Pongeroos had been blown to. They had landed right in the middle of Farmer Hendriks' manure heap!

'Good grief!' said Dan. 'Even if I can catch them they're going to stink to high heaven when I get them back to the Zoo.'

But watching the Pongeroos squealing with joy in the nasty, sticky mess gave Dan an idea.

Dan went to see Mrs Hendriks in the farm kitchen. 'I want to make the foulest, stinkiest, most horrible stew in the world!' said Dan. 'Can you help?'

Mrs Hendriks was delighted to help, and so they threw into her biggest pan all the pongiest ingredients they could find – fish heads, dirty socks, cabbage peelings, bad eggs and cowpats! It smelt so disgusting that Dan and Mrs Hendriks used clothes pegs to hold their noses.

When the stew was cooked Dan backed out of the
kitchen with the pot slurping and bubbling in front of
him. He walked across the farmyard towards the
Pongeroos in the manure heap. When they got the first
whiff their eyes lit up. They loved it!

Dan said goodbye to Farmer and Mrs Hendriks, loaded
the stew on to the back of the truck, and set off down
the road with the Pongeroos following close behind.

He drove to the harbour and put the truck on to the next ship for home.

Unfortunately the only ship left was too small to fit everyone in. Dan had to think fast, because the harbourmaster was getting angry. 'Get that smelly herd out of there!' he shouted.

Suddenly Dan had an idea. The Pongeroos could swim behind the ship! That way they would get washed clean by the time they reached the other side.

The Pongeroos followed Dan and the filthy-smelling stew all the way back to the Monster Zoo. They live to this day in a big cage between the Zoo kitchen and the garden, so they can sniff the cooking and the flowers.

Once in a while the postman brings a special delivery from Mrs Hendriks in Holland as a little treat for the Pongeroos.

Dan even found another use for the smelliest stew in the world...

It keeps all the bugs off his prize roses!

Other books in the Monster Zoo series include:

# THE GREAT BAMBOOZLE BIRD
# THE ENORMOUS BLOB
# THE SPOTTY FINGERSNITCH